This Book Belongs To

_____

To Mommy, Daddy,
Mairav & Aynat who
believed in me even
when I didn't always.

And reminded me to
proofreed my work.

Idan

it takes patience

First published 2019

Text © Idan Ravin 2019
Illustrations © Alison Mutton 2018

ISBN 978 1 7341713 0 3 (Hardcover)
ISBN 978 1 7341713 1 0 (Paperback)
ISBN 978 1 7341713 2 7 (e-book)

Typeset in Duper Pro 16pt.
Graphic design by Alison Mutton
Alene Illustration | alene-art.com

www.ittakespatiencebook.com

It Takes Patience

By Idan Ravin

Illustrated by Alison Mutton

I love Nana.
She always waits for me at the
bus stop after school.

"Hurry, Pumpkin! I've got cornbread baking in the oven. Next time, you'll bake some with me!"

"Yippee!"

"Nana, how come your food always tastes so yummy?"

"My Nana taught me to put *love* in my *food*, and my *food* in the *people I love*."

"Can you teach me?"

"I can, like I taught Momma."

Right before Thanksgiving, Nana makes
cornbread like I've never seen her do before.

"Watch closely, Pumpkin," she says.

"How long do I stir, Nana?"
"Just as long as your eyes
tell you to."

"How much sugar and salt, Nana?"
"Trust your fingers."

"How many corn kernels do we add, Nana?"
"Only your heart knows."

A few days later Nana says she's going away for the winter.

"Where are you going?"
"Down South. This cold weather is too hard on these old bones."
"Nana, dinosaurs have old bones. You have *new* bones."

"Remember your cornbread when I'm away," says Nana.

I hug Nana like I hug my blankie
during a bad storm.

"Are you hungry, sweetheart?" asks Momma.

"Not so much."

"How about if we make Nana's cornbread?
I think I remember," Momma says.

"I guess we can try."

Momma has her recipe in front of her, and all these measuring
spoons and cups.

Nana just uses her fingers.

Momma's so serious when she measures and mixes the ingredients.

Me and Nana laugh and play when we're in the kitchen.

Momma tells me to hush and keep still because she needs to focus.

Nana says her spoons make beautiful music.

Momma sets a timer I didn't even know we had.

Nana says Heaven pokes her on the shoulder when her cornbread's ready.

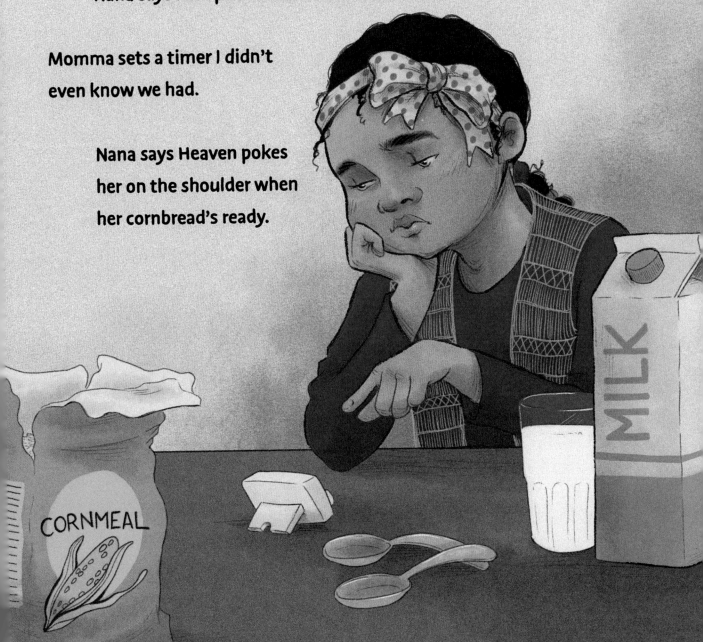

Momma cuts me a piece. I give my dog, Precious, some of mine.

"It's okay," I say, "just different."

"Not like Nana's, huh? Is it okay if we give it another try tomorrow? I'm really tired from work today."

"Fine," I whisper.

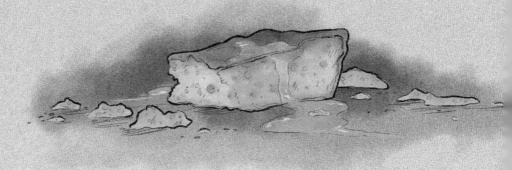

"Momma, I'm gonna make you a pinky promise. I'm gonna make the most perfect cornbread ever for Nana when I see her this spring."

"It doesn't have to be perfect, sweetheart."

"No, Momma. It's gonna be perfect, just perfect. I promise, Momma. I double pinky promise."

"We can't keep all our promises. Heaven knows, I couldn't keep that promise to Nana when I was younger."

"Why?"

"Because life got in the way."

"A promise is a promise!"

I shout.

Every day after school, I try to make cornbread, but the crust burns, the bread crumbles, and it won't rise. I even use too much grease.

"Momma, I'm afraid."
"Of what, sweetheart?"
"That I won't keep my promise, no matter how hard I try."

"How much do you love Nana?"
Momma wonders.

"This much!" I shout
as I spread my arms out
as far as I can.

"Good!" Momma says.
"Because that's what
it's going to take to
make your
cornbread
sing."

One night I can't sleep at all. Nana says on those nights that Heaven's my alarm clock, and I should wake up to do the first thing that comes to mind.

"Momma! Momma! Wake up, wake up!"
"What's wrong, Patience?"
"My promise to Nana."

I hold the spoon *gently*, like Nana's hand.

I play with the batter *softly*, the way Nana does my hair.

And I *smile the whole time*, because Nana says never
to make cornbread when angry
'cause people can taste it.

My crust comes out *crispy and the color of gold*.
It doesn't make a mess when I pull it apart.
And the honey *dances* on top of the bread.

"Momma, what's wrong?"
"Nothing, my love. It reminds
me of ... Nana's."

Even Precious is happy.

I wake up really early 'cause
the birds are singing. I feel just like the birdies.
Today's going to be the *best day ever*,
better even than my birthday.

I hear a knock on the front door.

"Nana!"

I run to the door *faster than I've ever run.* Faster even than when I raced the rain.

I hug Nana *tighter than I've ever hugged my blankie.*

"Pumpkin, I missed you."
"I missed you too! Guess what, Nana? I've got a **surprise** for you!"

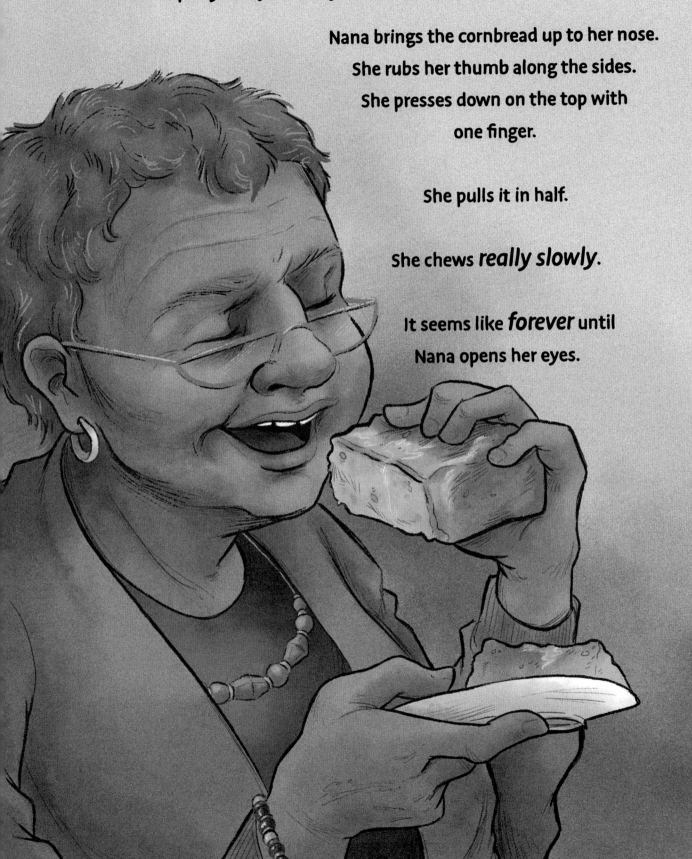

"Something smells *scrumptious*!"

"You can't open your eyes until you taste it, okay?"

Nana brings the cornbread up to her nose.

She rubs her thumb along the sides.

She presses down on the top with
one finger.

She pulls it in half.

She chews *really slowly*.

It seems like *forever* until
Nana opens her eyes.

"Pumpkin, did Momma help you make it?"

"No, Nana. She watched and I baked."

"How did you make it?"

"I just tried to do it like you."

"That's all?" Nana wonders.

"I also thought about *you smiling*, and Precious' tail going *straight up in the air* when she's happy, and *Momma's tears*, and the cornbread looking like *gold* with insides *better than candy*, singing on the plate.

And I thought about my promise to you and Momma."

"Pumpkin, your cornbread doesn't taste like mine."

"But I did everything I was supposed to."

"You did even more."

"I don't understand, Nana."

Nana takes my hand and we walk to her big chair on the porch.
She sits down first. I sit next to Nana.

She wraps her
fingers around mine.

"Pumpkin, I didn't want you to find **MY** cornbread. I wanted
you to find **YOURS**, and you did."
"I did?"
"You certainly did! Now let's hurry back inside so we can get
working on that homemade strawberry jam!"

CORNBREAD RECIPE

"Anything is possible if we listen to the magical voice we have inside," Nana says.

I found MY cornbread and hope you'll find YOURS too.

HOW I MAKE MY CORNBREAD

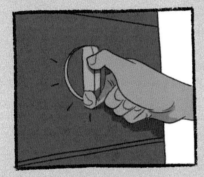

Momma pre-heats the oven for me to 350F.

In a large bowl, I use my hands to mix 1 cup cornmeal, 1 cup all-purpose flour, 1 tablespoon baking powder, 1/2 cup sugar, and 1 teaspoon salt.

I add 1 cup whole milk, 1/2 cup canned or thawed frozen corn kernels, 2 large eggs, 1/2 stick melted butter, and 1/4 cup of honey.

I mix it all together.

And, I smile the whole time!

I grease the muffin pan with butter or use cupcake liners before I pour in the batter to fill the liners 2/3 to the top, so there is room for the batter to rise in the oven.

I bake for 20 minutes if I make 12 medium-sized muffins, or 15 minutes if I make 24 mini-sized muffins. When the muffins are golden, I know they are ready.

I play hide and seek with Precious while it bakes.

Momma takes the cornbread out of the oven so it can cool.

I decorate my cornbread with any toppings I want, even cereal, like Froot Loops or Apple Jacks; sweets, like candy corn or M&M's; fruit, like blueberries or strawberries; and honey, Nutella, or icing that help the toppings stick on top.

TELL ME HOW YOU MAKE YOURS!

@ittakespatiencebook
#findyourcornbread
It Takes Patience Book
www.ittakespatiencebook.com

Made in the USA
Monee, IL
15 July 2020

Before Nana goes away for the winter, seven-year-old Patience makes her a unique promise. But no matter how hard Patience tries, perfection always seems beyond her grasp.

Can Patience look within to find the creativity, love and resilience she needs to keep her promise? Certain to capture the eyes and ears of children, and the hearts of parents, *It Takes Patience* teaches us all that anything is possible once we learn to listen to the magical voice we have inside.

About the Author

Idan Ravin's debut children's book draws on more than a decade of experience training NBA and WNBA superstars and explores the themes he developed in his first work, *The Hoops Whisperer* (Penguin, 2014). Idan's ability to transform athletes into their best selves translates itself into a new medium in *It Takes Patience*, offering inspiration and wisdom for children and parents alike. Along with being a proud and devoted uncle to his nieces and nephew, Idan's literary and coaching work has been featured extensively in the *Wall Street Journal*, *Sports Illustrated*, the *New York Times*, the *New Yorker*, the *Boston Globe*, *Men's Health*, and *Men's Fitness*, among others.

$12.9
ISBN 978-1-7341713-1-
5129

9 781734 171310

Today's Okay

by
Jacob M. Cheha

illustrated by Mark Pagano